SAM'S BALL

SAM'S BALL

Barbro Lindgren
illustrated by Eva Eriksson

William Morrow and Company
New York   1983

English translation copyright © 1983
by William Morrow and Company
Original copyright © 1982 by Barbro Lindgren (text)
and Eva Eriksson (illustrations).
First published in Swedish
by Rabén and Sjögren, Stockholm, Sweden,
under the title *Max Boll*.

Printed in the United States of America.
1 2 3 4 5 6 7 8 9 10

Library of Congress Cataloging in Publication Data
Lindgren, Barbro. Sam's ball.
Translation of: Max boll.
Summary: Sam and his cat clash over
who gets to play with the ball.
[1. Balls (Sporting goods)—Fiction.
2. Cats—Fiction]
I. Eriksson, Eva, ill. II. Title.
PZ7.L65852Sab 1983 [E] 83-722
ISBN 0-688-02359-2

SAM'S BALL

Look, here's Sam.
Look what's in Sam's bag.

Sam has a ball.

Sam plays with the ball.

Here comes Kitty.
Meow. Meow.

Kitty takes Sam's ball.

Kitty plays with Sam's ball.

Bad Kitty!

Sam wants the ball.

Kitty falls down.
Meow. Meow.

Sam takes the ball.

Kitty wants to play with Sam.
Good Kitty!

Kitty can play with Sam.
Sam and Kitty can play.

other books about Sam

SAM'S BATH

SAM'S CAR

SAM'S COOKIE

SAM'S LAMP

SAM'S TEDDY BEAR